D1266717

ALFONSO CASAS

MONSTER MIND

ABLAZE

ALFONSO CASAS

MONSTERMIND

ABLAZE

FOR ABLAZE

Managing Editor
Rich Young
Editor
Kevin Ketner
Design
Rodolfo Muraguchi

Translation by
Andrea Rosenberg

Lettering by
Taylor Esposito

Special Thanks to
Paula Prats and Alba Adell

Publisher's Cataloging-in-Publication data

Names: Casas, Alfonso, author.
Title: Monstermind : dealing with anxiety and self-doubt / Alfonso Casas.
Description: Portland, OR: Ablaze Publishing, 2021.
Identifiers: ISBN: 978-1-950912-47-6
Subjects: LCSH Casas, Alfonso--Comic books, strips, etc. | Cartoonists--Spain--Biography--Comic books, strips, etc. | Mental health--Comic books, strips, etc. | Anxiety--Comic books, strips, etc. | Comics (Graphic works) | BISAC COMICS & GRAPHIC NOVELS / Nonfiction / Biography & Memoir | COMICS & GRAPHIC NOVELS / Nonfiction / General
Classification: LCC PN6737.C378 M66 2021 | DDC 741.5--dc23

Monstermind. Published by Ablaze Publishing, 11222 SE Main St. #22906 Portland, OR 97269.

For advertising and licensing email: info@ablazepublishing.com.

10 9 8 7 6 5 4 3 2 1

CAN YOU TELL ME WHEN IT ALL STARTED?
WELL... I'M NOT SURE...

I GUESS THERE'S NOT REALLY AN EXACT MOMENT...
...AT LEAST NOT ONE I CAN PINPOINT.

IT CREEPS UP ON YOU GRADUALLY, WITHOUT YOU EVEN NOTICING.
IT'S SUBTLE, YOU THINK YOU'RE JUST GOING ON AS USUAL...
...AND NOTHING'S CHANGED.

UNTIL ONE DAY YOU REALIZE YOU'RE TRAPPED...

...AND BY THAT POINT YOU HAVE NO IDEA HOW TO GET OUT.

I've always been a bit of a
slow starter when I wake up.

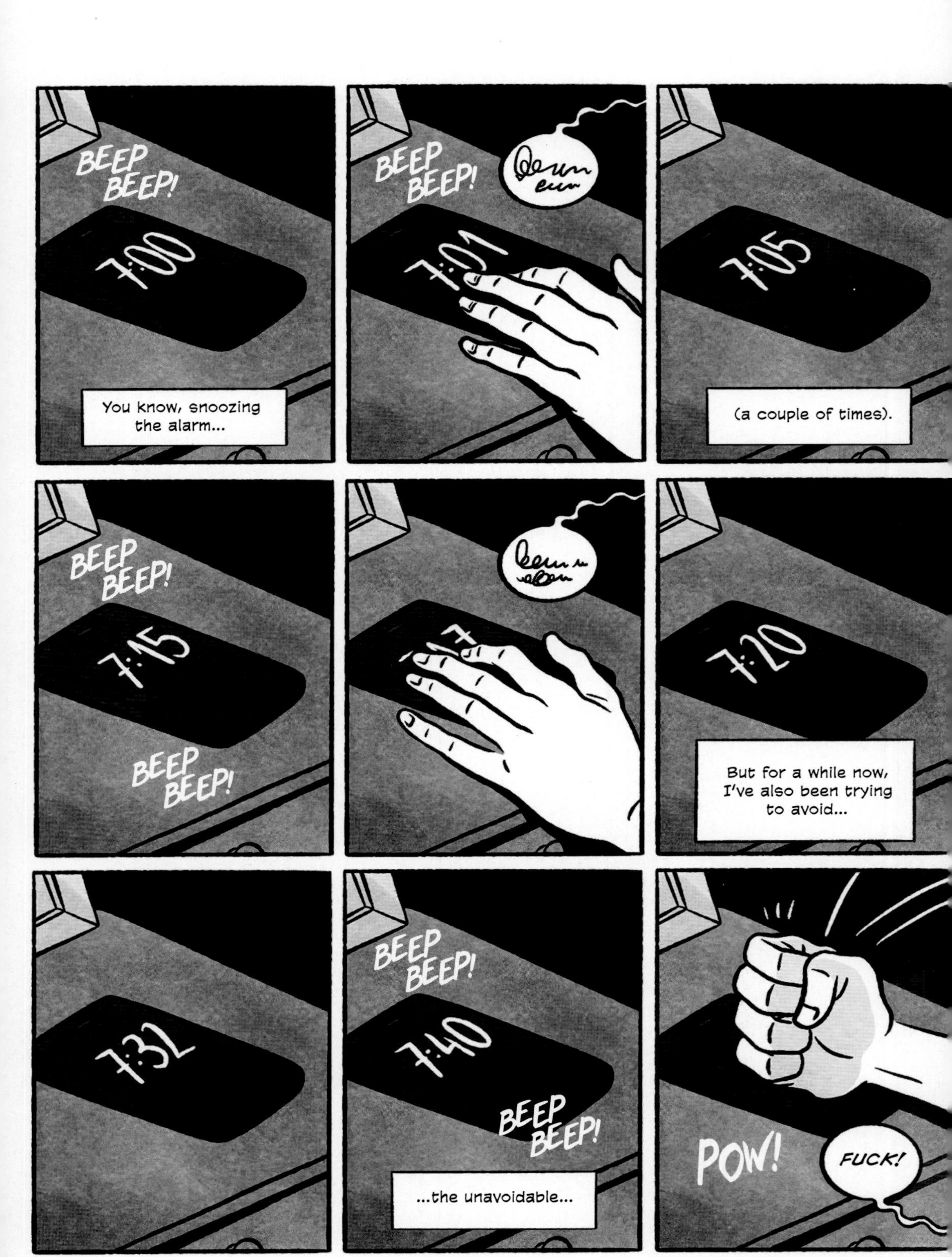
BEEP BEEP!
7:00
You know, snoozing the alarm...
BEEP BEEP!
7:01
7:05
(a couple of times).
BEEP BEEP!
7:15
BEEP BEEP!
7:20
But for a while now, I've also been trying to avoid...
7:32
BEEP BEEP!
7:40
BEEP BEEP!
...the unavoidable...
POW!
FUCK!

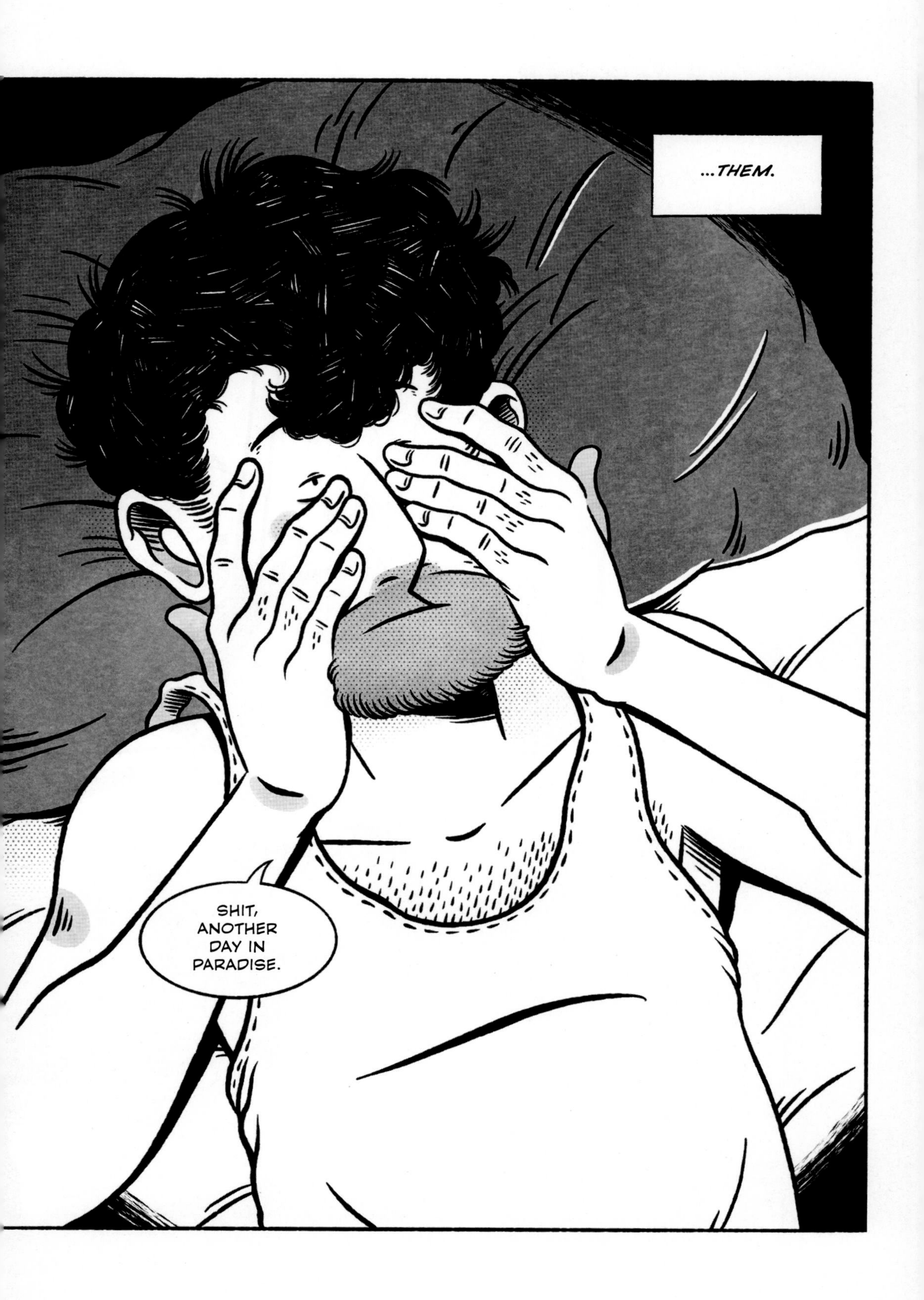
...THEM.
SHIT, ANOTHER DAY IN PARADISE.

WOULD YOU GUYS LEAVE ME ALONE!
SOMEBODY WOKE UP ON THE WRONG SIDE OF THE BED.
GGR

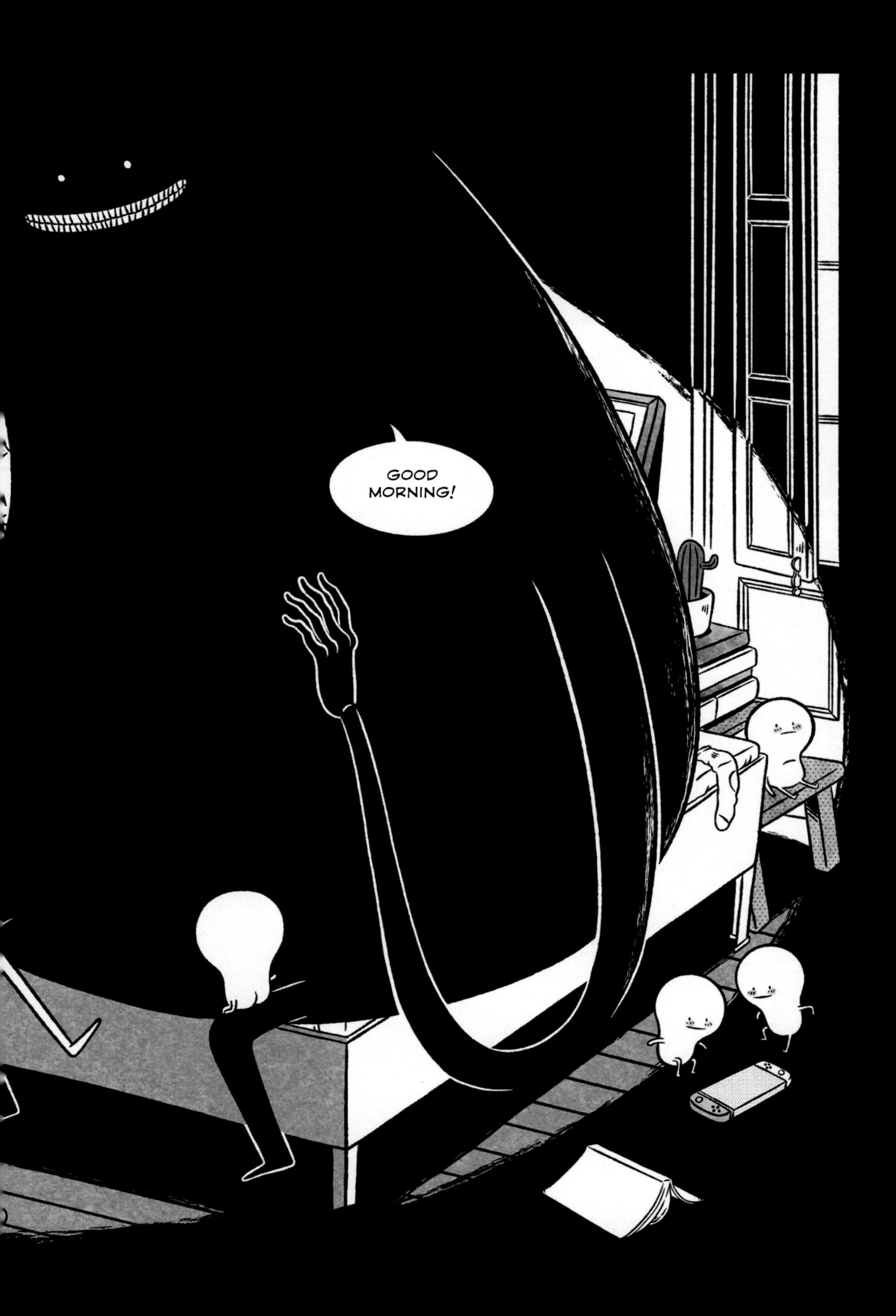
GOOD MORNING!

8:10 A.M.
HAVE YOU HAD A LOOK AT THAT MOLE THERE?
GET OUT!!!

8:30 A.M.
WHAT DO YOU WANT FOR BREAK-FAST?
INTEGRAL Anxieties
Regret'os
0% useful
HELP
I'M GOOD WITH COFFEE, THANKS...

9:00 A.M.
I'D CHANGE THIS RIGHT HERE.
WHICH PART?
ALL OF IT.

1:30 P.M.
SERIOUSLY? EVERYWHERE I GO?

7:30 P.M.
YOU'RE A TOTAL SQUARE...
I WONDER HOW LONG BEFORE EVERYBODY REALIZES.

9:00 P.M.
SINCE 1981
TOMATO KETCHUP
BEER

DID YOU THINK IT FILLED ITSELF?

11:00 P.M.
DON'T EVEN THINK ABOUT IT! NO HOGGING THE COUCH.

ARG!
YOU'RE SUFFOCATING ME!

MOVE!
OUCH!
WHAT? ROUGH DAY?
...

MONSTER
MIND

My balcony is exactly 26 inches wide.
THE HAIR
Since I live in a 430 sq ft studio, I suppose the balcony's "proportionate."
But I can't complain.
If you're flexible enough, you can enjoy 45 fleeting minutes of direct sunlight.

One day, rereading an old comic I ran across while clean- ing...

...I found a tiny hair between its pages.

It could have been an eyelash or a hair from an eyebrow.

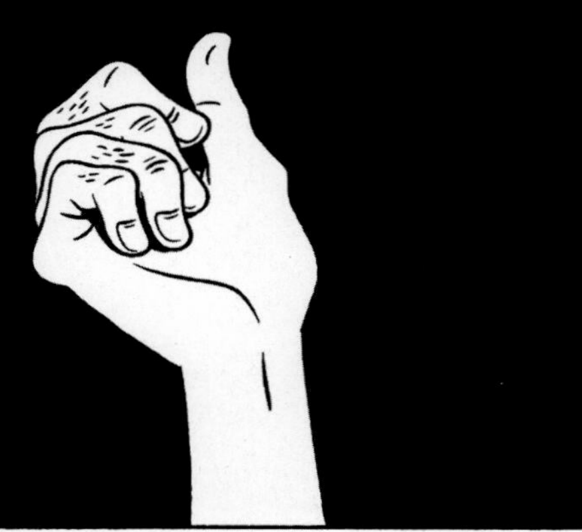
Or maybe the first time I read it I had short hair (and hadn't yet had to grow bangs to hide my receding hairline).

What was that "me" like back then?

WHEN DO YOU THINK IT'S FROM?
???
NOT A CLUE, HONESTLY.
I HAVEN'T READ IT IN A LONG TIME...
©2004
YOU WERE PROBABLY A LOT YOUNGER.
GGRR!
I ALREADY KNOW THAT!

WHAT ARE YOU GUYS TALKING ABOUT?
JUST WHAT I NEEDED...
HE FOUND AN OLD HAIR AND IT SEEMS LIKE HE'S GETTING ALL PENSIVE.
SWIPE!
OH? LET'S SEE IT!
WHAT WERE YOU LIKE BACK THEN? WE WEREN'T AROUND...
WELL, THEN I WAS HAPPIER, OBVIOUSLY...

WHAT WOULD YOU WISH FOR?
THAT THE DREAMS YOU HAD BACK THEN WILL COME TRUE?
ARE YOU CLOSER TO RESEMBLING THE PERSON YOU WANTED TO BE THEN...
...OR THE ONE YOU FEARED BECOMING?

GIVE IT!
SWIPE!

FFFSHH!

FFFSHH!

WHOOSH!

WHEN IN DOUBT

They started out harassing me at night.

They'd show up just before I fell asleep.
ZZZ...
ZZZ...

(Well, sometimes a little after...)

HEY THERE.
??

WHO ARE YOU?

I'M THE DOUBT YOU FEEL ABOUT WHETHER YOU SHOULD'VE DONE THAT THING YOU DID.

UM, OKAY...

...I UNDERSTAND EVERYTHING NOW.

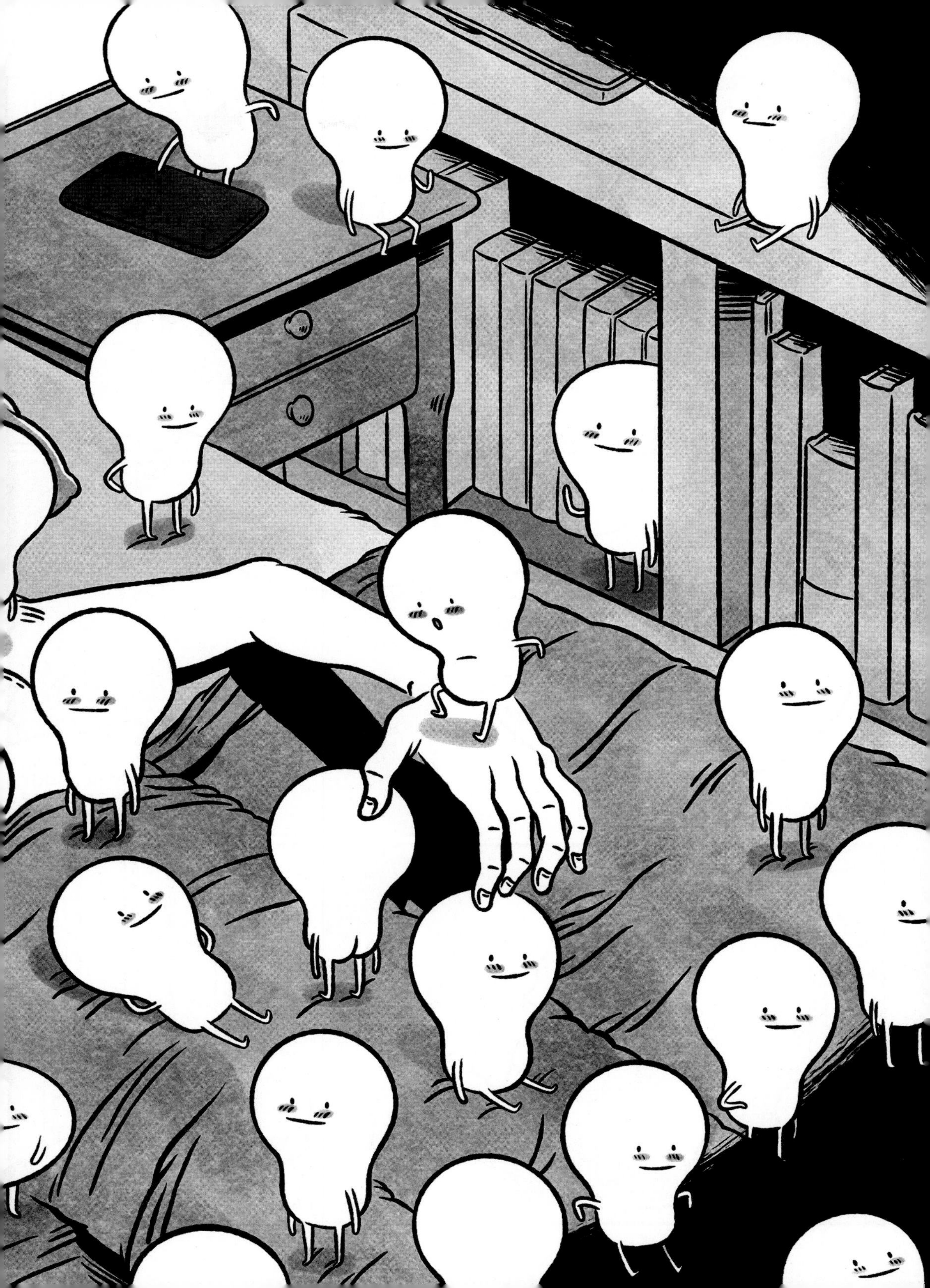

AND WHO ARE YOU?

YOU DON'T LOOK LIKE THE OTHERS...

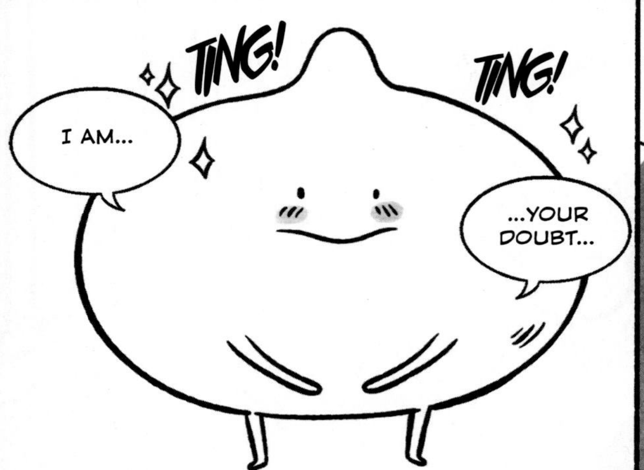
TING!
TING!
I AM...
...YOUR DOUBT...

...ABOUT THAT THING YOU DIDN'T DO...
...AND WILL WONDER ABOUT FOR THE REST OF YOUR LIFE.

YOU...

YOU'RE THE WORST OF ALL.

SOLD TO THE BEST IMPOSTER
MMM...
Received (0)
NOT A SINGLE EMAIL, HUH?
Email
Search
Compose
Unread
Received (0)
Starred
Sent
SEEMS LIKE YOU HAD YOUR MOMENT...
BUT CLEARLY THIS ISN'T IT.
WELL, YOU GUYS PROBABLY HAVE SOMETHING TO DO WITH THAT!
HOW DID YOU GO FROM "YOUNG PROMISE" TO "OLD GLORY" WITHOUT THE GOOD STUFF IN BETWEEN?
WHOOSH!
LOOK HOW GREAT THINGS ARE GOING FOR "X"...CLICK ON THEIR PROFILE!

THEY'RE ALWAYS DOING THINGS... THEIR INBOX MUST BE OVER-FLOWING!
REMINDS ME OF YOU A FEW YEARS BACK...
ALL RIGHT, THAT'S ENOUGH!
EVERYBODY'S ON THEIR OWN PATH...
IT'S DIFFERENT, NOT BETTER!
THE IMPORTANT THING IS TO KEEP LOOKING AHEAD...
...NOT TO THE SIDE TO SEE IF YOU MEASURE UP.
CLAP!
CLAP!
CLAP!
WOW, WHAT A GREAT SPEECH...
GGRR!
I'M SURE "X" WOULD HAVE DONE IT BETTER...
He always gets the last word.

WHATEVER YOU WANT
17:03
online
TODAY
Hey! Feel like doing something tonight?
7:31 p.m.
absolutely! i'm in!
7:32 p.m.

Would you rather go out or should we stay in?
whatever you want!
We can watch a movie...or if you want we could binge a TV show.
ok, whatever you want!
What do you want for dinner? We could order pizza, or sushi!
you choose, whatever you want!
GGRR!
LOOK, YOU KNOW WHAT...?
YOU NEED TO TELL HIM...
TIC! TIC! TIC!

WELL, YOU KNOW THE OLD SAYING: "IT'S BETTER TO BE ALONE THAN IN BAD CO--"

SHUT UP!!!
SLAP!
Sometimes I manage to end up alone and in bad company.

THIS FRIDAY IS SERGIO'S BIRTHDAY AND HE'S HAVING A PARTY AT HIS HOUSE...
IT'S THE PERFECT OPPORTUNITY TO SEE ALL MY FRIENDS...
AND
I'M GOING.
Monday
BOGGED

Tuesday
I'M GOING.
Human Times
MONSTER Daily

Wednesday
I'M GOING!
SKROOCH, SKROOCH!

Thursday
I...AM...

Friday
SERGIO? YEAH, LISTEN, TURNS OUT I'M A NO-SHOW TONIGHT, I GOT BOGGED DOWN WITH THIS THING AND WON'T BE ABLE TO MAKE IT.
I KNOW, I FEEL TERRIBLE...

"The thing"

HAPPY?
Social anxiety: 1 - Me: 0

I WISH EVERYBODY WOULD LEAVE ME ALONE...
MY TWO PER

FUCK, I'M SO LONELY.
TUAL MOODS

WHERE THE $#&%! DID YOU GUYS COME FROM?

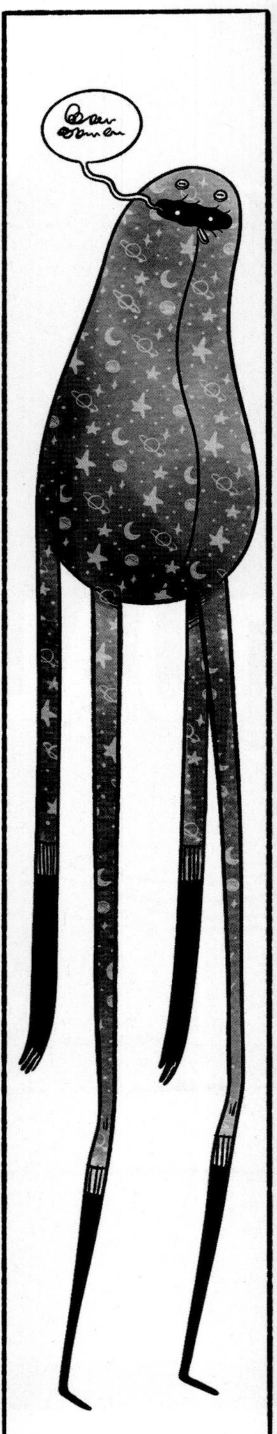

I ARRIVED AROUND THE TIME HE SIGNED HIS FIRST CONTRACT.
SINCE THEN, IT'S BEEN MY MISSION TO REMIND HIM THAT SOONER OR LATER EVERYBODY'S GOING TO REALIZE HE'S AN IMPOSTER.
I DON'T REMEMBER THE FIRST TIME I SHOWED UP...
...BUT WHENEVER I DO, HE FEELS TOTALLY LOST. I CAN'T HELP IT.
I ALWAYS SHOW UP WITHOUT WARNING.
LOOKS LIKE IT'S GOING TO RAIN...
MY STORY'S ON THE NEXT PAGE.

As a kid I was obsessed with this toy that was on display in a shop window near my house...
Whenever I walked by, I couldn't take my eyes off it.
It was the most incredible-- and unnerving--toy I'd ever seen:
a bird that never stopped drinking.
I couldn't understand how the thing worked...
To me it was just magic.

Some become sweet childhood memories, while others...

...become little traumas that stay with you forever.
CAN YOU BRING ME ANOTHER?
WHY DON'T YOU EVER STOP DRINKING?!
YOU FINISHED THEM ALL!
WELL, YOU COULD GO OUT AND BUY MORE, RIGHT? COME ON, BE A SPORT.

THE GREAT DIVIDE
KUK, KUK!

ARE YOU OKAY? YOU SEEM OFF...
SURE, I'M FINE...

YOU SURE?
I'M SURE.

...

The small earthquake we had that day
shook the earth and split it apart,

leaving the
two of us
KUK. KUK!
on either side
of the abyss.

BOOM!
BOOM!
BOOM!
SADNESS

Never dismiss someone who tells you they're sad...
...by telling them they need to feel better.*
*Believe me, that's already occurred to them.
And don't tell them they have no reason to be sad either.
That's the awful thing about sadness:
you may think the reason isn't real...

...but the sadness definitely is...
PLIC!
PLIC!
PLIC!
WHO'S THIS GUY?

PLIC!
PLIC!
PLIC!
PLIC!
NO IDEA.
HE SHOWS UP SOMETIMES, THE WAY STORMS DO. HE VENTS FOR A WHILE AND LEAVES...

GUYS, HE FELL ASLEEP AT THE TABLE. WHAT SHOULD WE DO?
DRAW ON HIS FACE WITH A MARKER?

What is this?

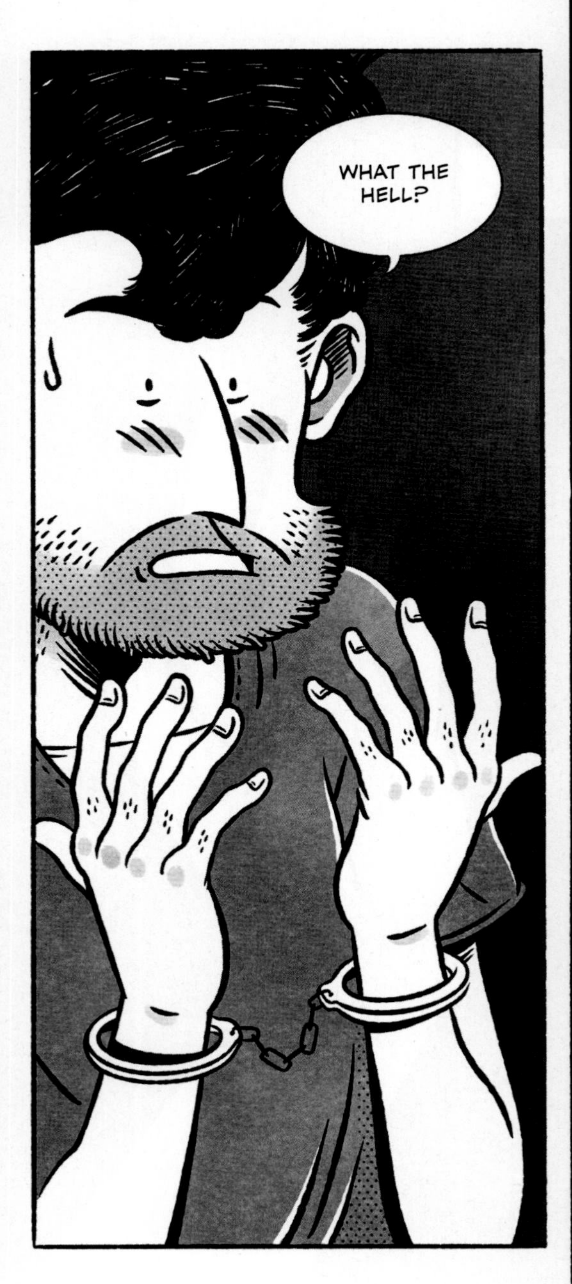
WHAT THE
HELL?

THE TRIAL
WHERE AM I?! ?!?!
WHAT DO YOU KNOW ABOUT THIS?
RELAX, EVERYTHING'LL GO FINE.

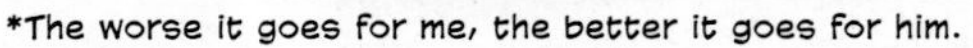
*The worse it goes for me, the better it goes for him.

HEY!
HI!
WHO ARE THESE GUYS? SOME OF THEM LOOK FAMILIAR, BUT THE REST...
COME ON, COME ON, LET'S GO.
I HAVEN'T BEEN ON INSTAGRAM YET TODAY AND I'VE ALWAYS GOT A TON TO DO THERE...
YOUR ESTEEMED HONOR!
YEAH, YEAH, CLOSE THE DOOR. THERE'S A DRAFT.
YOU... YOU'RE THE JUDGE?
CAN YOU THINK OF A BETTER CHOICE, GIVEN HOW MANY YEARS WE'VE KNOWN EACH OTHER?
LET'S SEE WHAT WE HAVE HERE... CASE 270681...

THE WORLD VS. YOU!
BAM!

BUT I HAVEN'T DONE ANYTHING!

THAT'S THE PROBLEM, YOU HAVEN'T DONE ANYTHING...
YOUR HONOR, I ACCUSE THIS MAN OF LEADING A MEDIOCRE LIFE!
THIS ISN'T WHAT WE'D PLANNED FOR OUR FUTURE!
DAMN, HE REALLY TAKING IT SERIOUSLY

COULD IT BE THAT WE HAD TOO MUCH HOPE FOR THE KID?
MAYBE IT'S TIME TO LOWER OUR EXPECTATIONS...

I OB-JE-CT!

DO YOU OBJECT TO SOMETHING THE JUDGE SAID?
WHAT DO I KNOW, YOUR HONOR? THIS IS A DREAM, AND EVERY-THING I KNOW ABOUT TRIALS I LEARNED FROM WATCHING *ALLY McBEAL*.*
AHEM, AHEM!
*Please don't ask me to explain what *Ally McBeal* is, you're making me feel old. Just Google it.
WHAT I MEAN IS, LOWERING EXPECTATIONS IS A COWARDLY MOVE.
WE COULD ASPIRE TO MORE WITH THE CARDS WE'VE BEEN DEALT.
IT'S HIS FAULT HE'S PLAYED THEM BADLY.
ALL RIGHT, IF THIS IS A DREAM, I WANT TO WAKE UP.
GAH!
IT'S TRUE HE'S BEEN IN A RUT FOR A WHILE NOW.
I CAN HEAR YOU!
SO WHAT ARE YOU SUGGESTING, THEN? WHAT SHOULD HIS PUNISHMENT BE?
PLOP!

I SUGGEST A RADICAL CHANGE.
...OR WHEN HE BOUGHT THAT LEATHER JACKET...
BUT NOT LIKE THAT TIME HE BLEACHED HIS HAIR...
THAT'S A LOW BLOW.
A REAL LIFE CHANGE.
BOOM!
I KNOW THINGS HAVE MAYBE BEEN A BIT OF A DISASTER LATELY, BUT... WHAT CAN I DO?
I CAN'T CHANGE JOBS AND I CAN'T LEAVE THE CITY.
MY WHOLE LIFE IS HERE!

WHAT LIFE?
BLAH, BLAH, BLAH...
BLAH, BLAH, BLAH...
BLAH, BLAH...

ORDER! ORDER!
THOCK, THOCK, THOCK!
I'M SURE THE LAWYER FOR THE DEFENSE MUST HAVE SOMETHING TO SAY.
GREAT. TOP-NOTCH DEFENSE.

YOUR HONOR, THE ACCUSED HAS CONSISTENTLY FAILED TO LIVE UP TO EVERYTHING HE PROMISED.
WHERE'S THAT MORTGAGE HE WAS GOING TO GET BEFORE THIRTY?
AND THOSE PROMISES OF PROFESSIONAL SUCCESS?
NOT TO MENTION THE "SELF-CONFIDENCE" HE WAS SUPPOSED TO ACHIEVE WITH AGE.
THUNK
THUNK
THUNK

HE DOESN'T EVEN KNOW HOW TO AINTAIN A ROMANTIC RELATIONSHIP...!
THAT'S TRUE.

WHAT I'M TRYING TO SAY, YOUR HONOR, IS THAT THIS GUY RIGHT HERE IS...

AN IMPOSTER!!!

I KNEW IT!

SWIPE!
MOST ESTEEMED MEMBERS OF THE JURY, THIS ISN'T A QUESTION OF EXPECTATIONS.

THE ACCUSED DOESN'T KNOW THE DIFFERENCE BETWEEN LIVING...

...AND EXISTING.
MIC DROP!

NOTHING FURTHER, YOUR HONOR.
CLAP! CLAP! CLAP!
CLAP! CLAP!
CLAP!
CLAP! CLAP!
CLAP!
CLAP! CLAP!
CLAP! CLAP!
CLAP!
CLAP!
CLAP!
CLAP!

ORDER IN THE COURT! I'LL ASK THE JURY NOT TO CLAP FOR JUST ONE OF THE PARTIES. AT LEAST FAKE IT A LITTLE!
THE ACCUSED IS LOOKING A LITTLE DEFLATED, I SEE. ARE YOU ALL RIGHT?
AND YOU, GIVE BACK MY GAVEL RIGHT THIS MINUTE. I DON'T WANT TO BREAK MY FLASK!
THOCK, THOCK, THOCK!
AM I ALL RIGHT, HE ASKS...
OH!
OF COURSE I'M NOT!
I HAVEN'T BEEN ALL RIGHT SINCE YOU GUYS SHOWED UP!
IT'S NOT THESE HANDCUFFS THAT HAVE ME TRAPPED, IT'S ALL OF YOU!

HOW CAN I FINISH THE THINGS ON THAT LIST WITH THIS GUY ALWAYS HANGING AROUND?
I HAVEN'T OPENED MY MOUTH THIS WHOLE CHAPTER...

AND YOU, ALWAYS BROODING ABOUT THE FUTURE! YOU WORRY ABOUT THINGS EVEN WHEN YOU HAVE NO IDEA IF THEY'RE GOING TO HAPPEN!

AND YOU, DON'T THINK I DON'T RECOGNIZE YOU. I KNOW PERFECTLY WELL WHO YOU ARE.
IT'S IMPOSSIBLE TO LOOK AHEAD WHEN YOU'RE ALWAYS REMINDING ME ABOUT THE PAST!

WHEN THE PAST IS SO EVER-PRESENT, IT'S NOT THE PAST ANYMORE, IT'S THE PRESENT!
??
IT SOUNDS LIKE A TONGUE-TWISTER, BUT I GOT IT...

WHAT I MEAN IS, I'M SO TORMENTED BY THE PAST...
...AND SO WORRIED ABOUT THE FUTURE...
I CAN'T FOCUS ON THE PRESENT!
HUH, HE'S NOT WRONG.
YEAH, THESE GUYS ARE PRETTY HARD ON HIM...
QUIET!
THOCK, THOCK, THOCK!
I'VE BEEN WITH YOU SINCE YOU WERE FIVE, AND NOW YOU WANT ME TO LEAVE?
AT LEAST A LITTLE VACATION...

THIS IS CONTEMPT OF COURT, ACCUSING THE JUDGE OF ONE'S OWN CRIME!
TAKE HIM AWAY!!!
WAIT!
LET ME EXPLAIN! STOP!
STOP!!!
STOOOOOP

PPP!
GASP!
DAMN, WHAT A CRAZY NIGHTMARE. LUCKILY IT WAS ALL A...
OOF!

...DREAM.

I'VE GOT TO DO SOMETHING.

THE CIRCLE OF (NO) LIFE
YOU'VE BEEN WORKING ALL DAY, YOU SHOULD TAKE A BREAK...
YOU SHOULD BE WORKING...

SHOULDN'T YOU GET SOME EXERCISE?
HUFF, HUFF!
YOU SHOULD SOCIALIZE A LITTLE.

TOXIC
ALL RIGHT, MESSAGE SENT.
TIC! TIC! TIC!

PLIC!
??

HE READ IT, BUT HE'S NOT ANSWERING.
PLIC!
PLIC!

DID I SAY SOMETHING WRONG?
WHY DID I SEND THAT, I'M THE WORST...
PLIC!

SHIT, HE'S PROBABLY MAD AT ME FOR SOMETHING AND DECIDED HE ISN'T INTO ME.

I'M SUCH A JERK
WHY DIDN'T I KEEP MY MOUTH SHUT?
IT'S ALL BECAUSE I'M AN IDIOT
I NEVER LEARN
WHO DO I THINK I AM?

Hey! I was at the movies.
What's up?

ARE YOU
HERE TO STAY?
EMPTY

PLOP!
KRAK!

ERROR:
THE PROGRAM CLOSED UNEXPECTEDLY
ACCEPT
ACCEPT
ACCEPT
THONK!

RRRRIP!

CLONK!

SCRIITCH!

ARE YOU HERE TO STAY?

WELL, LET'S SEE IF THEY CAN MAKE ROOM FOR YOU. WE'RE A LITTLE TIGHT ON SPACE.
...
HEY, NEW GUY! SINCE YOU'RE UP, CAN YOU BRING ME A BEER?

LITTLE BY LITTLE...

ARE YOU SEEING THIS?
YEAH, IT'S ON EVERY CHANNEL...
DO YOU WANT ME TO LEAVE?
ACTUALLY, THEY'RE SAYING WE CAN'T GO ANYWHERE...
"WE'LL CONTINUE TO BRING YOU THE LATEST ON THE..."
PANDEMIC

PLUS, IT DOESN'T SEEM RIGHT...
"...WE GO NOW LIVE TO THE PRESIDENT'S ANNOUNCEMENT ON THE STATE OF EMERGENCY..."
I DON'T KNOW...I'VE GOT MY HOUSEMATES, BUT YOU...
I FEEL BAD THAT YOU'RE ALL ALONE.
DON'T WORRY ABOUT THAT...

...I'M NOT GOING TO BE ALONE.

That's what started it all off: it was time to learn to live with them...
...or to kick them out once and for all.

AN
ORDINARY
DAY

WHAT ARE YOU DOING?
WHY ARE YOU ALWAYS POPPING UP OUT OF NOWHERE?!

I'M DRAWING A COMIC.
HEY! THAT'S US!
HEY! COME HERE! YOU GOTTA SEE THIS!

LOOK, HE'S MAKING A COMIC ABOUT US!
WOULD YOU ALL LEAVE ME ALONE?
A COMIC? DO YOU THINK PEOPLE WILL LIKE IT?
WELL, I DON'T KNOW, BUT I WANTED TO GIVE IT A SHOT.
WEREN'T YOU GUYS SAYING I NEEDED A CHANGE?
WHEN DID WE SAY THAT?
MAYBE HE DREAMED IT.
I SENSED MY PRESENCE WAS NEEDED HERE.
OH, GREAT...
IT'S ABOUT US!
SO, THIS IS WHAT YOU'VE BEEN UP TO...

SEEMS LIKE THIS WON'T TURN OUT WELL...
I DON'T THINK YOU'RE READY TO DRAW SOMETHING LIKE THIS...
IS THIS A GOOD MOVE, CAREER-WISE? I HAVE MY DOUBTS...
KRAK!

SLAM!
WILL ANYTHING I DO EVER BE GOOD ENOUGH FOR YOU GUYS?
...
...
...
NO.
ALL RIGHT, THAT'S IT.
I NEED YOU ALL TO LEAVE...
...FOREVER.

WHAT'S GOING ON? WHY ALL THE FUSS?
COME ON, LET'S CHILL OUT IN FRONT OF THE TV FOR A BIT. WE'LL MAKE ROOM FOR YOU ON THE COUCH.
WHOA, WHOA, LET'S CALM DOWN.
IF YOU DON'T LEAVE, I WILL.

HEY, WAIT A MINUTE!

WHAT IN THE WORLD DID YOU DO TO HIM?
TAP!
TAP!
TAP!
TAP!

YOU CAN'T LEAVE, YOU NEED US!
I DON'T WANT TO KEEP LISTENING TO YOU ANYMORE.
TAP!
TAP!

YOU SHOULD HAVE DONE IT.
IT WASN'T EVEN THAT HARD.
HAVE YOU SEEN YOURSELF, MAN?
ANYBODY COULD DO IT...EXCEPT YOU.
YOU SHOULDN'T HAVE DONE IT.
HE SA IT BECAU HE FEE SORRY F YOU.
WHY DID YOU SAY THAT?
BEST NOT EVEN TRY IT.
THEY'RE ALL GOING TO REALIZE NOW.
IT WAS PREDICTABLE.
IT'S BEST THEY DON'T SEE YOU.
WHAT IF THEY THINK I'M A JERK?
IS THIS THE BEST YOU CAN DO?
EVERYTHING COMES OUT IN THE END.
IT'S NOT PESSIMISM, IT'S REALISM.
THIS DOESN'T LOOK GOOD AT ALL.
NOW WHAT?
YOU'VE GOT TO PREPARE FOR THE WORST.
THE FUTURE IS HERE AND LOOK AT YOU.
YOU ONLY NEED TO SEE THE PAST.
MAKE A DECISION ALREADY!
YOU CAN'T GO ON LIKE THIS.

STOP
IT.

STOP
IT.

STOOOPPP!

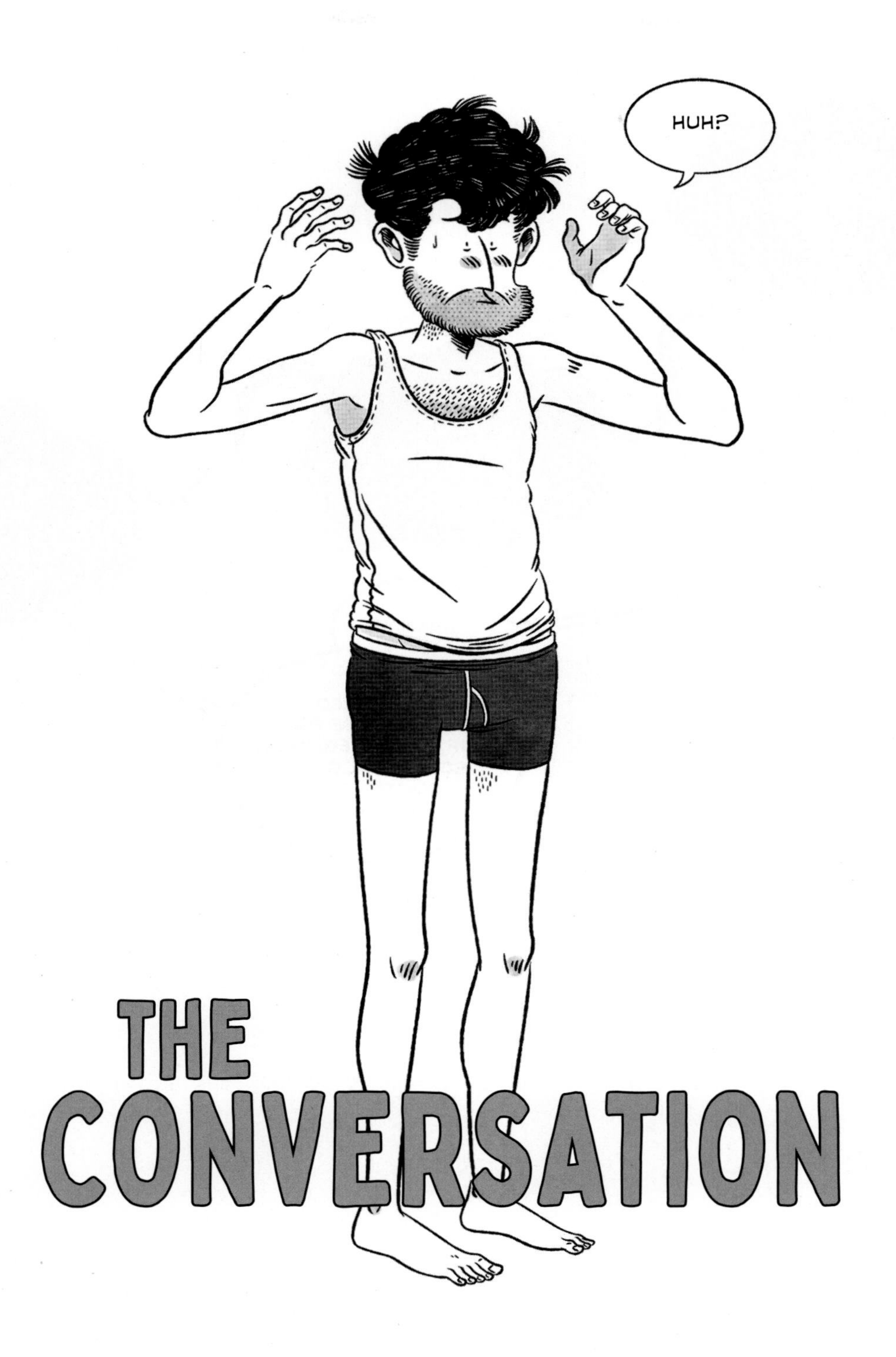

THE CONVERSATION

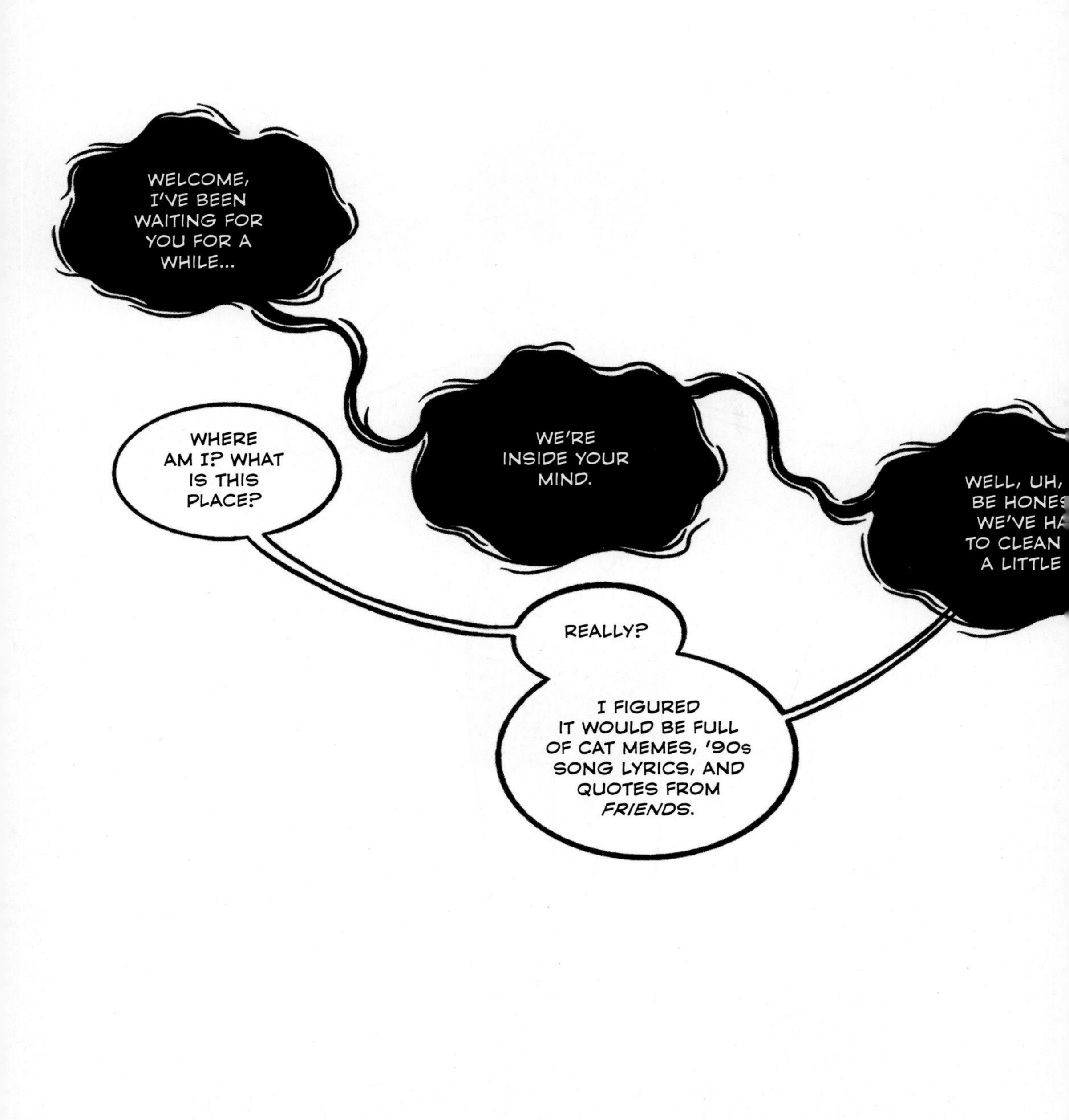

WELCOME, I'VE BEEN WAITING FOR YOU FOR A WHILE...
WHERE AM I? WHAT IS THIS PLACE?
WE'RE INSIDE YOUR MIND.
REALLY?
I FIGURED IT WOULD BE FULL OF CAT MEMES, '90s SONG LYRICS, AND QUOTES FROM *FRIENDS*.
WELL, UH, BE HONES WE'VE HA TO CLEAN A LITTLE

AND WHAT DID YOU DO WITH THE MONSTERS?
THEY WERE HERE A MINUTE AGO...
THEY STILL ARE.
??
I AM
ALL OF YOUR MONSTERS.

"ALL OF YOUR MONSTERS," HE SAYS.
THAT'S RIDICULOUS...

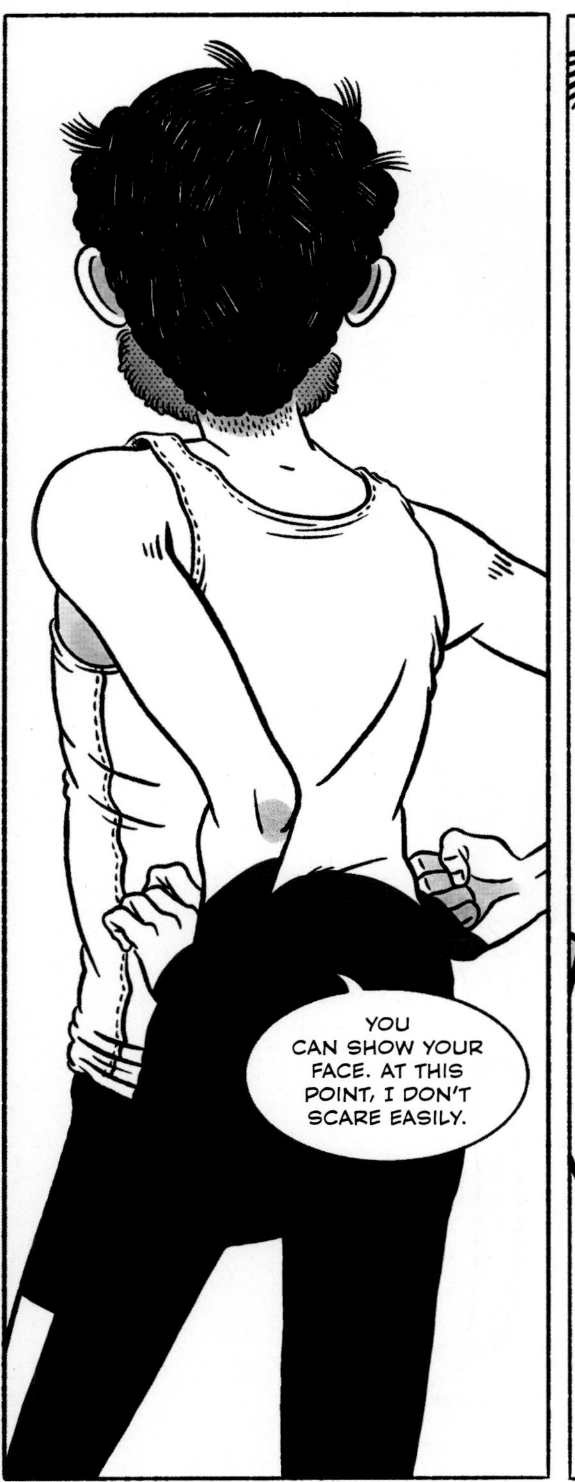
YOU CAN SHOW YOUR FACE. AT THIS POINT, I DON'T SCARE EASILY.

??
HHH...

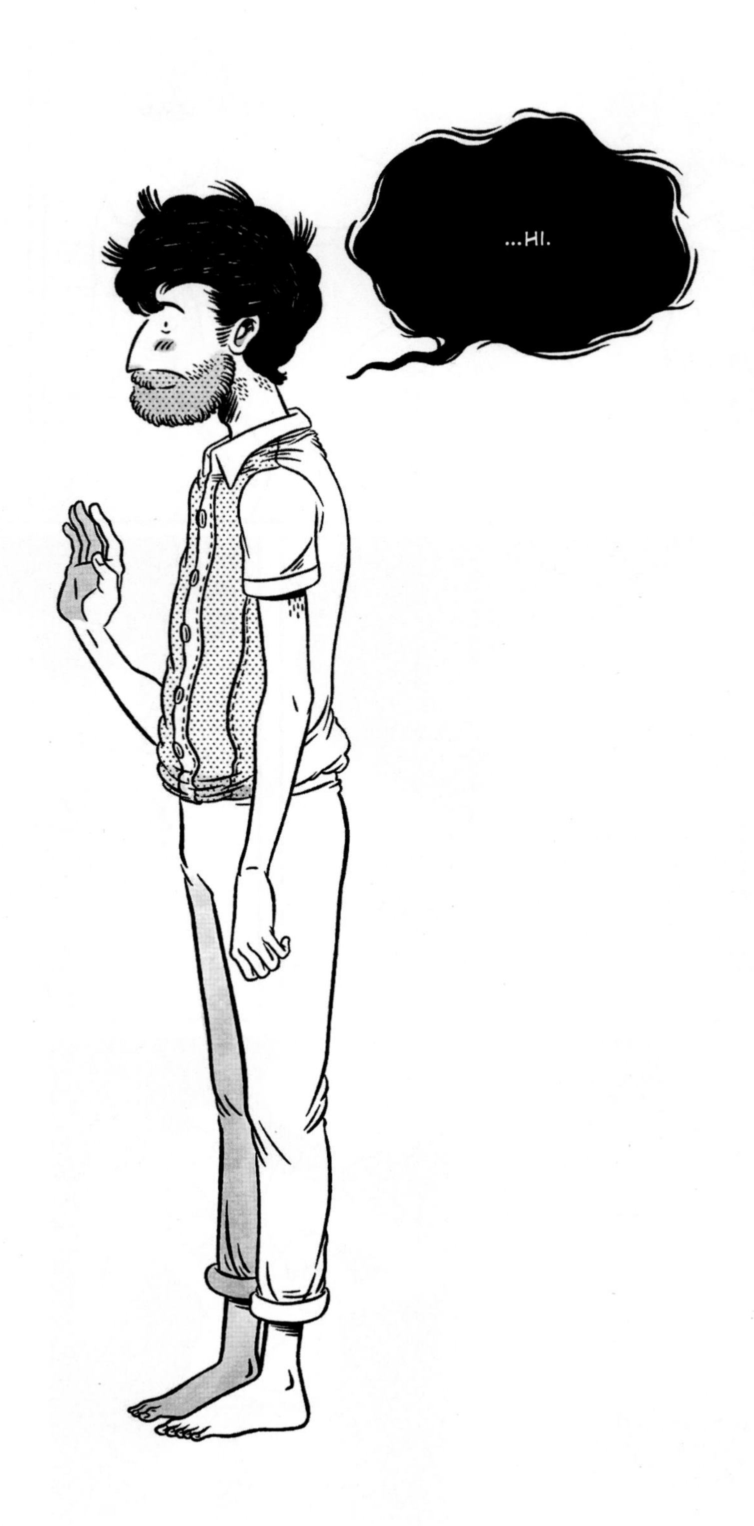
...HI.

YOU! I MEAN... ME!
WHO THE HELL ARE YOU?!
HA! HA! HA! HA!
I KNEW YOU'D FREA OUT.
I AM THE ORIGIN OF ALL YOUR MONSTERS.
I'M YOUR SHADOW.

MY SHA...

I'M DREAMING AGAIN...

COME ON, I WANT TO SHOW YOU SOMETHING...

WOW!
SO, THIS...I MEAN... IT'S...
...HE'S ME?
WELL, SORT OF...
HE'S MORE OF AN IDEALIZED VERSION OF YOU...
...THAT'S WHY HE HAS SUCH GREAT HAIR.
I SEE...
AND YOU SEE THAT SHADOW?
YES...

YOU BUILT THAT STATUE FOR YEARS, A VERSION OF YOU SO IDEALIZED THAT IT WAS--OBVIOUSLY--UNATTAINABLE.
IDEAL
PROTECTION
DISTANCE
YOU
AND IN THE GAP BETWEEN YOU AND THAT IMAGE OF YOU, A SHADOW WAS CAST...
...WHICH IS WHERE ALL MONSTERS COME FROM.

WELL, SEE, THAT SHADOW...

...IS ME.

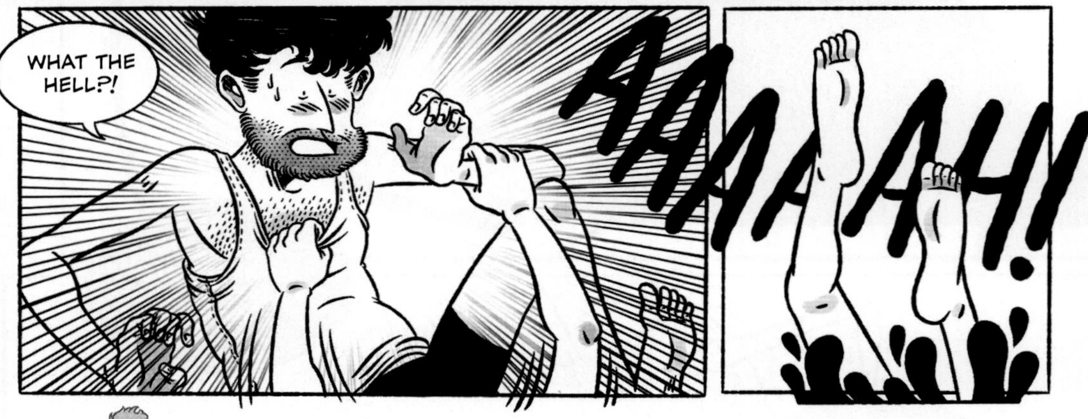
WHAT THE HELL?!
AAAAAAH!

SPLASH!

SO, SINCE YOU CREATED THOSE MONSTERS...
...CAN'T YOU MAKE THEM LEAVE?
I HATE TO TELL YOU THIS, BUT...
YOUR MONSTERS AREN'T GOING TO DISAPPEAR.
WHAT?
THUD!
COME ON.

YOUR MONSTERS ARE THE THING THAT HOLDS YOU BACK...
FOR EXAMPLE:
"IT'S IMPOSSIBLE TO DO ANYTHING WHEN THEY'RE ALWAYS WORKING AGAINST ME."
...AND, AT THE SAME TIME, THE PERFECT EXCUSE TO NOT EVEN TRY.
YOU'RE ALL LIKE:
"THEY'RE ALWAYS TRIPPING ME UP, SO I'M OUT."
YOU DO A TERRIBLE IMPRESSION OF ME. I DON'T "TALK LIKE THAT."

THESE MONSTERS ARE PART OF YOU.
THEY'LL ALWAYS BE IN THE WAY.

BUT YOU CAN MAKE SURE THEIR IMPACT ON YOU GOES FROM BEING LIMITING...

TO BEING LIMITED.

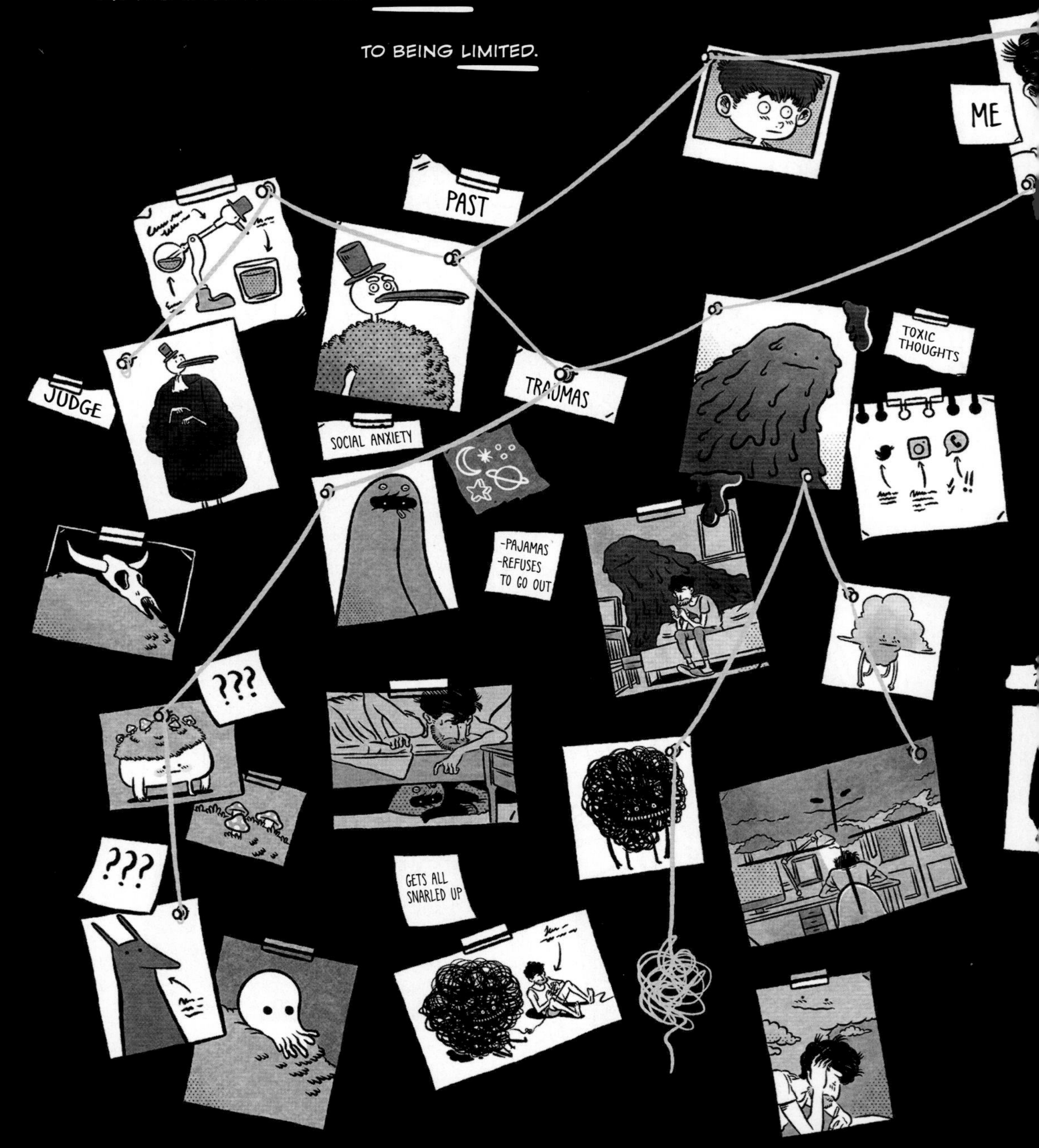

ACCEPTING YOURSELF, WITH ALL YOUR STRENGTHS AND YOUR...WELL, THEM!

DO YOU UNDERSTAND? (I MAY HAVE GOTTEN A LITTLE CRYPTIC...)

I THINK SO.
GREAT, BECAUSE I'VE GOTTA GO.

CAN'T YOU STAY A LITTLE LONGER? I'VE GOT SO MANY QUESTIONS!

RELAX. FROM NOW ON...

...I'M HERE FOR YOU.

THANKS.

I THINK WE'VE MADE GREAT PROGRESS THE LAST FEW SESSIONS, WOULDN'T YOU AGREE?
WE REALLY HAVE...
SHALL I PUT YOU DOWN FOR ANOTHER IN THREE WEEKS?
PERFECT.

Little by little. I realized it was futile to try to get rid of them...
...because we're all chased by our own monsters.
Even people who don't seem to have any...
...most likely...

...are trying to figure out how to deal with them, too.
Learning to live with your monsters is a path you'll be on your whole life...
...but that's the challenge, right?
Until one day...
THAT'S WEIRD...

WHY IS IT SO QUIET? EVERYTHING'S SO CALM.

Just kidding, they're still here...FOR NOW.
HEY, CAN YOU LET ME IN? I LOCKED MYSELF OUT...
YOU GUYS ARE GETTING WORSE AND WORSE AT HIDING...
WELL, THIS APARTMENT'S STILL ONLY 430 SQ FT, RIGHT?

This isn't the triumphant
tale of a hero who
defeated his monsters...

BEEP BEEP!
7:00
BEEP BEEP!

7:01

...it's just the story of somebody...

...who's learning to live with them.
SORRY, I CAN'T SLEEP IN. I'M IN A HURRY.

YOU'VE GOT THAT IMPORTANT MEETING TODAY, HUH?
YOU KNOW WHAT THEY'RE GOING TO SAY, RIGHT?
I DON'T KNOW ABOUT THEM, BUT YOU FOR SURE...

THANKS.
I'D WEAR THE BLACK ONE, IT'S SLIMMING.
HOP!
YOU'RE STAYING HERE...
WANT ME TO COME WITH?
NOT TODAY.

YOU GUYS STAY PUT, YOU GET THE WHOLE COUCH TODAY!
WHY DON'T YOU STAY? AFTER ALL, YOU KNOW...
YEAH, YEAH, I KNOW. WISH ME LUCK!

PICK UP SOME BEER ON YOUR WAY HOME!
GOOD LUCK...
BYE!
SLAM!

ANYWAY...
HOO...

THE KID'S REALLY GROWING UP, HUH?
I'M NOT GOING TO CRY, I'M NOT GOING TO CRY...
HE'S A REAL SUPERSTAR, I'VE ALWAYS SAID SO.
THE END

You know when something happens that suddenly sets all your internal alarms bells ringing? Well, it's almost always this monster who presses the red button.

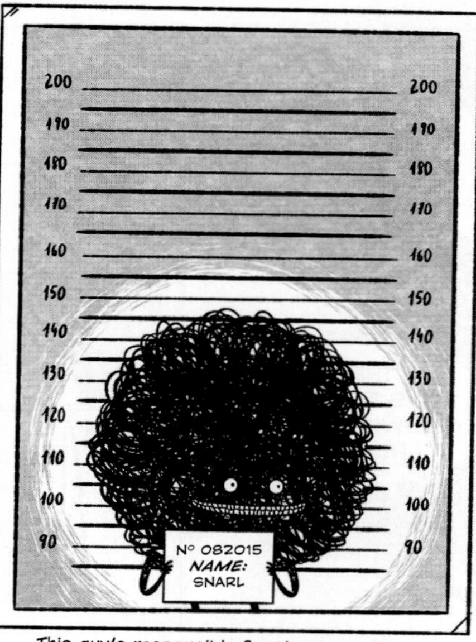

This guy's responsible for those constant little defeats that make your days a slog.

Don't be fooled by how cute they are; these mini-monsters are the worst. Especially dangerous at night and when they show up in a pack.

The worst thing about this monster is that "once you pop, you can't stop." This guy can contaminate everything around him. Cleaning him out is hard, but not impossible.

Thinking about the future is such a gri activity, he'll use any means necessar to keep you busy in the present worryi about what's to come.

Like a good deodorant, this monster never abandons you. Sometimes he's small and doesn't get in your way, but other times he grows huge and paralyzes you.

It's not just that he doesn't like leaving the house, he never even sticks his head out of his pajamas (which is why you can barely understand him when he talks). If you're wavering between going out and staying home to watch TV, this monster has the answer.

His greatest obsession is convincing you that it's just a matter of time before the world figures out you're a fraud. This monster's a real prize.

Ever have one of those days where, without really knowing why, all you want to do is re-watch The Bridges of Madison County or listen to Adele? This monster won't be far away.

(Many remain unclassified still.)

To all the people who are part of
my life, thank you for putting up
with my monsters while you're
also dealing with your own.

MONSTERMIND

MONSTERMIND
DISCUSSION GUIDE

MONSTERMIND: DEALING WITH ANXIETY & SELF DOUBT BY ALFONSO CASAS
DISCUSSION GUIDE BY **MATTHEW NOE, MSLS**

SYNOPSIS
Alfonso is dealing with some rather unpleasant guests that, no matter how hard he tries, simply will not leave. As if that weren't bad enough, these guests are actually monsters living inside of his head and contributing to the stress of millennial life during a global pandemic. From the nightmarish bird-toy-come-alive Mr. Past Traumas to the, frankly, adorable Doubts and countless unnamed monsters in between, Alfonso's emotions push him nearly to the breaking point – until it finally becomes clear what he's *really* struggling against. *MonsterMind* is an honest examination of living with anxiety and the fears of never being enough that will speak to an entire generation.

MAJOR CHARACTERS
Alfonso, Mr. Past Traumas, Snarl, Doubts, Toxic Thoughts, Anxiety about the Future, Fear, Social Anxiety, Imposter Syndrome, Sadness, Sergio

THEMES
Mental Health, Anxiety, Doubt, Acceptance

DISCUSSION QUESTIONS

1. *MonsterMind* opens with an unseen character, in what appears to be a professional setting, asking Alfonso when "it" all started. By the end of the text, it becomes clear what this setting is. What is this setting and why do you think he chose to leave it vague?

2. In "The Hair," Alfonso finds a small hair in a comic book from his childhood, causing him to become, as Fear calls it, pensive. Do you think this is an accurate description of the emotions he is feeling? Why pensive rather than nostalgic?

3. "Never dismiss someone who tells you they're sad by telling them they need to feel better." This, hopefully obvious, advice is rather important to keep in mind. What are some better ways to help someone who is struck by a seemingly invisible sadness?

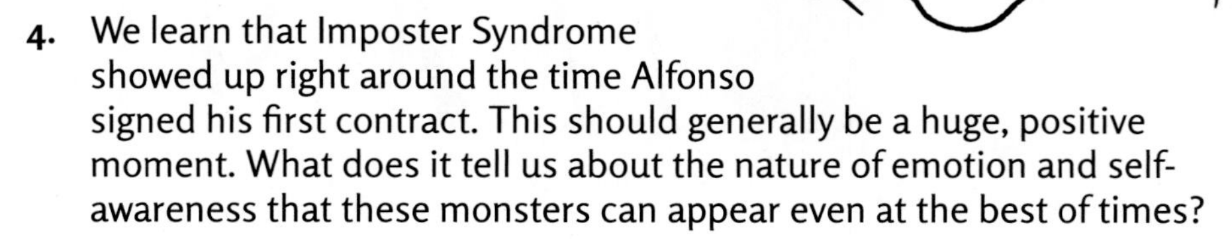

4. We learn that Imposter Syndrome showed up right around the time Alfonso signed his first contract. This should generally be a huge, positive moment. What does it tell us about the nature of emotion and self-awareness that these monsters can appear even at the best of times?

5. The monsters appear in a number of forms, some clearly defined and others a bit more unclear. What does the appearance, or form, of the monster convey about what they represent?

6. Mr. Past Traumas is easily the most defined of the monsters in terms of appearance. Why might that be the case? Do you have a "certain childhood experience" that has become etched in your brain?

7. Mr. Past Traumas, based on a toy bird that never stops drinking, is shown in one panel to still have a need to constantly drink. Is this simply a continuation of childhood memory or does it indicate something more?

8. During The Trial, Anxiety About the Future suggests that lowering expectations for oneself is an act of cowardice. How do you feel about this claim?

9. Alfonso is accused of not knowing the difference "between living and existing." Is there a difference, and if so, what is it?

10. "When the past is so ever-present, it's not the past anymore, it's the present." Rightly described as a tongue-twister, what exactly is Alfonso trying to say here? Might there be an answer to how to live inside this claim?

11. *MonsterMind* is broken into a series of shorter stories (not quite chapters). How does this arrangement impact the flow of the larger story?

12. The emergence of the COVID-19 pandemic marked a turning point for Alfonso's relationship with his monsters – how could it not with the forced need for isolation? How did the pandemic impact your mental health and relationship with your own monsters?

13. Alfonso's Shadow emerges to explain that he, and all the monsters, emerge out of the gap between an unobtainable, idealized version of himself. Does this metaphor work for you? Do you have a different way of understanding the origins of your own monsters?

14. "This isn't the triumphant tale of a hero who defeated his monsters... it's just the story of somebody who's learning to live with them." Alfonso is open about the source of his monsters and their impact on him, but it is this ending that may be the most honest part of the comic. What does it mean to learn to live with one's monsters? Do you think it is truly impossible to leave them behind, that anxiety, self-doubt, and all the other trappings of mental health struggles are lifelong?

PROJECT IDEAS

- Practice observing your own state of mind by recording a journal every day for a week or two, making note of the weather, your mood(s), your triumphs and struggles, and the day's activities. Feel free to write about these observations in prose, but also be certain to include illustrations or short comics as well. At the end of your observation period, reflect on what you've recorded. Did you learn anything new? Did any patterns emerge? Do any of your observations inspire you to make changes?

- Loneliness, though not a defined monster for Alfonso, is an ever present force in *MonsterMind*. Consider preemptively combating this powerful stressor by joining a local community organization and volunteering. You might consider getting involved with your local library and offering to coordinate a book club!

- Expressing emotion and mental health struggles in the form of monsters has a long history in comics and *MonsterMind* does this to great effect. Choose two or three defining feelings from your own life and create a monster mug-shot for them in the style found at the end of *MonsterMind*. If you're feeling particularly creative, create a short comic showing how these monsters all interact with one another to impact your life.

- Objects from the past play a large role in *MonsterMind*, to the point of inspiring the appearance of one of the monsters. Choose an object from your own past that holds special meaning (positive or negative) and create a 2 page comic about the origins of that object's meaning to you. Give special consideration to what emotions the object evokes in you and how those feelings have changed over the course of your life.

alfonso casas

alfonsocasas

anxiety
doubts
fears
insecurities
traumas
The tree that doesn't let you see the forest